A
Rookie
reader®

Field Day

Written by Melanie Davis Jones
Illustrated by Albert Molnar

Children's Press®
A Division of Scholastic Inc.
New York • Toronto • London • Auckland • Sydney
Mexico City • New Delhi • Hong Kong
Danbury, Connecticut

Rookie
READY TO
LEARN

Dear Parents/Educators,

Welcome to Rookie Ready to Learn. Each Rookie Reader in this series includes additional age-appropriate Let's Learn Together activity pages that help your young child to be better prepared when starting school.

Field Day offers opportunities for you and your child to talk about the important social/emotional skill of relating to others.

Here are early-learning skills you and your child will encounter in the *Field Day* Let's Learn Together pages:

• Rhyming
• Patterns
• Counting

We hope you enjoy sharing this delightful, enhanced reading experience with your early learner.

Library of Congress Cataloging-in-Publication Data

Jones, Melanie Davis.
  Field day/written by Melanie Davis Jones; illustrated by Albert Molnar.
    p. cm. — (Rookie ready to learn)

  Summary: Children have a wonderful time participating in the various activities of their school's field day.

  ISBN 978-0-531-27176-6 (library binding) — ISBN 978-0-531-26826-1 (pbk.)

  [1. Racing—Fiction. 2. Contests—Fiction. 3. Schools—Fiction.] I. Molnar, Albert, ill. II. Title.

  PZ7.J7235Fi 2011   [E] —dc22   2011010239

Acknowledgments
© 2003 Albert Molnar, front and back cover illustrations, pages 3–36, 37 children, 38–40. Page 35: © iStockphoto/Thinkstock. Page 39: © iStockphoto/Thinkstock, Brand X Pictures/Thinkstock, John Foxx/ Thinkstock.

1 2 3 4 5 6 7 8 9 10 R 18 17 16 15 14 13 12 11

Running fast.
Walking slow.

3

On your mark.

Mom and Dad smiling proud.

Clapping hands.
Cheering crowd.

Egg and spoon.

Relay races.

Drinks and snacks.

17

Painted faces.

Hula hoop.

Balloon pop.

Toss the ball.

Time to stop!

Way to go.
Hip, hip, hooray!

What a great field day!

Congratulations!

You just finished reading *Field Day* and learned how much fun it can be to join in when a community gets together for a special time.

About the Author
As an elementary school teacher, Melanie Davis Jones has participated in many field day events throughout the years. Mrs. Jones lives in Georgia with her husband and three sons.

About the Illustrator
Albert Molnar is an award-winning illustrator from Ottawa, Ontario, Canada. In his spare time, he enjoys spending time with his children, Sabrina and Tyler, and his wife, Danica.

Field Day

Let's learn together!

In Our Community

(Sing this song to the tune of "The More We Get Together.")

It's great to get together, together, together,
It's great to get together with our community.

We clean up on Earth Day,
We march on parade day.

We do so much together
In our community.

PARENT TIP: Participation in community activities gives children a sense of belonging and can provide an early introduction to civic engagement. Encourage your child to take an active part in her community with activities such as helping collect canned goods for a holiday food drive, attending a story hour at the local library, or spending an afternoon at a local block fair.

Field Day Fun

The kids in the story had a great time on field day.
They did many different activities together.

Say each action word in the top row. Then point to the word that rhymes with it.

go	clap	run

map	bow	sun

PARENT TIP: This activity helps your child build skill in recognizing letter and word sounds. After he finishes, read the book again. This time, emphasize each of the rhyming words (*slow/go, proud/crowd,* etc.) as you and your child enjoy the story again together.

Find the Shapes

▽ **triangle**

◯ **circle**

▢ **square**

☆ **star**

The children had their faces painted on field day. Look at the shape pictures and trace each one with your finger. Then find something in the picture that is the same shape. For example: The girl's eyes are circles.

PARENT TIP: Help your child build language skills. Encourage her to name the different shapes she sees as she completes this activity. Then go back through the book together and have her hunt for circles and stars in the story. This will support her shape-recognition skills, as well as her ability to notice details in pictures.

Relay Race!

Help the boy in the story finish the race.
Trace the path with your finger as you
follow the numbers in order from 1 to 10.

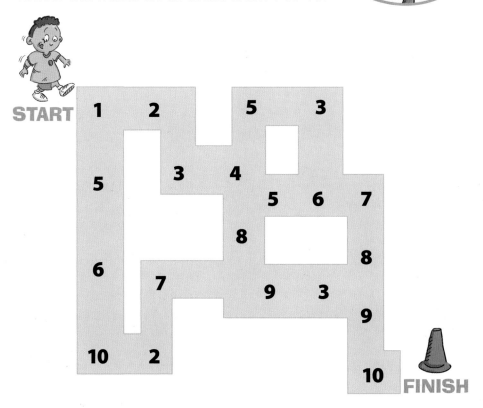

START 1 2 5 3

5 3 4

5 6 7

8

5 6

8

6 7 9 3

9

10 2

10

FINISH

PARENT TIP: As your child follows the path, he will be building
skill in problem solving, number recognition, and counting, as
well as left-to-right progression—an important prereading skill.

What Comes Next?

All day long the kids had fun. Look at each row. Say what comes next in each pattern.

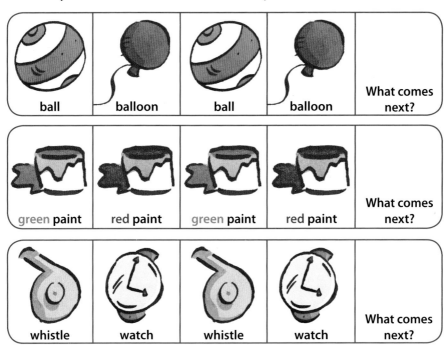

ball	balloon	ball	balloon	What comes next?
green paint	red paint	green paint	red paint	What comes next?
whistle	watch	whistle	watch	What comes next?

PARENT TIP: As your child identifies what comes next in this patterning activity, he will be building important problem-solving and early math skills. After enjoying the activity, go back through the book and help him become a better "picture reader" by hunting for a ball, balloon, paint can, whistle, and watch in the story.

Snack Time

The children in the book ate healthy snacks on field day.

Point to each slice of fruit in the top row. Then point to the whole fruit it comes from in the bottom row.

 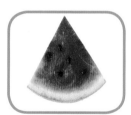 

PARENT TIP: Understanding part/whole relationships is an important early math skill. As your child matches each fruit slice to the whole fruit it belongs to, have her say the name of the fruit. Then go back to pages 16 and 17 in the story and have your child find these fruits in the picture. Ask your child to identify the carrot sticks, grapes, and cherries in the scene.

Field Day Word List (45 Words)

a	fast	on	stop
and	field	painted	the
ball	get	pop	time
balloon	go	proud	to
cheering	great	races	toss
clapping	hands	relay	walking
crowd	hip	running	way
Dad	hoop	set	what
day	hooray	slow	your
drinks	hula	smiling	
egg	mark	snacks	
faces	Mom	spoon	

PARENT TIPS:

For Older Children or Readers:
Write the word *running* from the word list on a piece of paper. Help your child identify the word, as well as the letters that make up the word. Then go back through the story and have your child identify the word in the text, as well as the picture that illustrates this action word. Continue with the remaining action words in the list.

For Younger Children:
Point to and share the word *running* from the word list with your child. Then go back through the book together to find someone running in the story. Continue this activity with the other action words in the list.